For Julia

I AM A GREAT FRIEND!

Lauren Stohler

Atheneum Books for Young Readers
New York London Toronto Sydney New Delhi

A family of capybaras lived at the edge of a big, cool pond.

On the muddy banks, they munched leaves with their soft gray snouts. They took long, luxurious naps. When the sun got hot, they floated peacefully in the water, swirling their cute webbed toes.

They went about their capybara business kindly and calmly, which made them perfect friends for the other animals who came to the pond to relax.

And nearly every capybara carried a bevy of birds on their back.

SO, WHERE'S MY BIRDS?

"Those things sound very fun,"
his mama said. "For you."

But if you want bird friends,
you have to do what birds like.

Float calmly.

Nap quietly.

And eat slowly.

"I CAM DO WAT," said Baby Capybara.

And he did. He chewed every mouthful of his
juicy green leaves one hundred times.

He floated so calmly that he didn't make a ripple.

And he napped so quietly
that when he woke up . . .

Baby Capybara's new birds were *beautiful*!
And there were so many!

He couldn't wait to show them
what a great friend he was.

Off they went–

rock climbing, hill rolling, pond jumping,

fruit squishing,
and capybara dodging!

Baby Capybara was so thrilled that he could barely feel the birds on his back!

It was as if they weren't there at all!

Oh.

They weren't.

AAAARRRGGGH!

cried Baby Capybara.

"I'm sorry about your birds," his mama said.
"Come snuggle."

No, said Baby Capybara.

I don't wanna.

I want to do fun stuff with them, like follow treasure maps and sing really loud and make mud pies.

I mean, who eats a whole mud pie all by themselves? It doesn't even taste good that way!

It's not fair!

WHY DOESN'T ANYBODY LIKE WHAT I LIKE?!

Baby Capybara felt sad. And lonely. And a little upset.

He watched everyone else enjoying their pretty, peaceful birds.

I AM NOT THE PROBLEM HERE,

he gurgled.

I AM **FUN!** I AM **FASCINATING!**
I AM A GREAT FRIEND!

plip!

You are *loud*.

So what?

I like it.

Look what I can do.

. . . can you play the drums?

Can you stealth wiggle?

CAN YOU BALANCE
A MILLION MELONS?

What is going on?   asked Baby Capybara's mama.

You will never get your birds back by being loud and splashy. Especially not with all those crocodile teeth nearby.

"I'm not a crocodile. I'm a caiman," said Baby Caiman. "I like long wriggles on the beach and hiding on logs, and my mother taught me never to eat my friends."

"That's very nice," said Mama.

But don't you want your birds,
Baby Capybara?

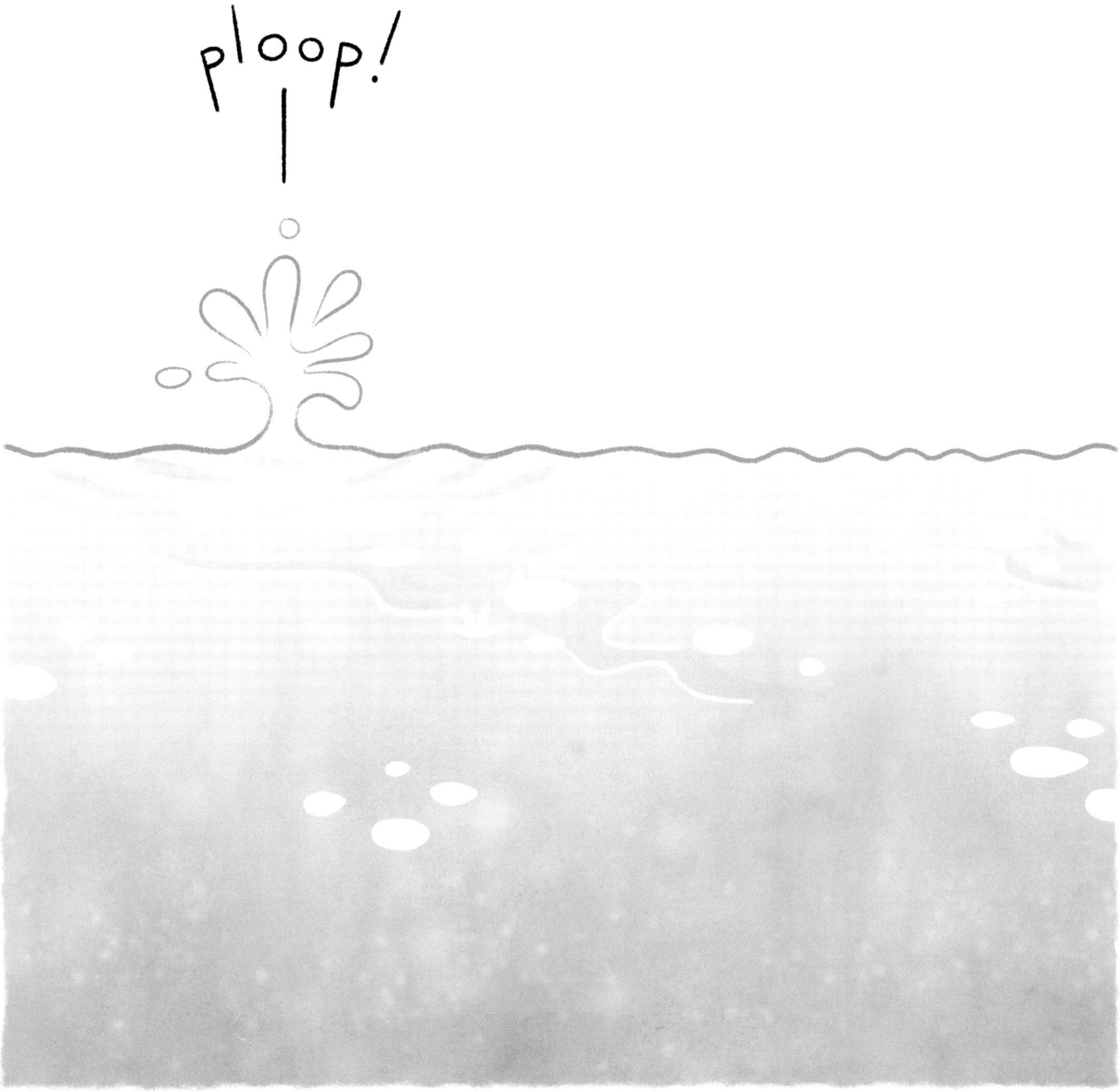
ploop!

ATHENEUM BOOKS FOR YOUNG READERS

An imprint of Simon & Schuster Children's Publishing Division
1230 Avenue of the Americas, New York, New York 10020

ATHENEUM BOOKS FOR YOUNG READERS is a registered trademark of Simon & Schuster, Inc.
Atheneum logo is a trademark of Simon & Schuster, Inc.
For information about special discounts for bulk purchases, please contact
Simon & Schuster Special Sales at 1-866-506-1949 or business@simonandschuster.com.
The Simon & Schuster Speakers Bureau can bring authors to your live event.
For more information or to book an event, contact the Simon & Schuster Speakers Bureau at
1-866-248-3049 or visit our website at www.simonspeakers.com.

The text for this book was set in Intro and Billy.
The illustrations for this book were rendered digitally.
Manufactured in Spain
1222 QUL

First Edition
2 4 6 8 10 9 7 5 3 1
Library of Congress Cataloging-in-Publication Data
Names: Stohler, Lauren, author, illustrator.
Title: I am a great friend! / Lauren Stohler.
Description: First edition. | New York : Atheneum Books for Young Readers, 2023. | Audience: Ages 4–8. | Audience: Grades 2–3. | Summary: Loud and splashy Baby Capybara must change his ways if he wants a bevy of peaceful birds perched on his back, but when an unexpected critter splashes onto the scene, he realizes he does not need to change himself to find friends. • Identifiers: LCCN 2022008530 | ISBN 9781665918336 (hardcover) | ISBN 9781665918343 (ebook) • Subjects: CYAC: Capybara–Fiction. | Animals–Fiction. | Individuality–Fiction. | Friendship–Fiction. | LCGFT: Animal fiction. | Picture books. • Classification: LCC PZ7.1.S7529 Iam 2023 | DDC [E]–dc23
LC record available at https://lccn.loc.gov/2022008530